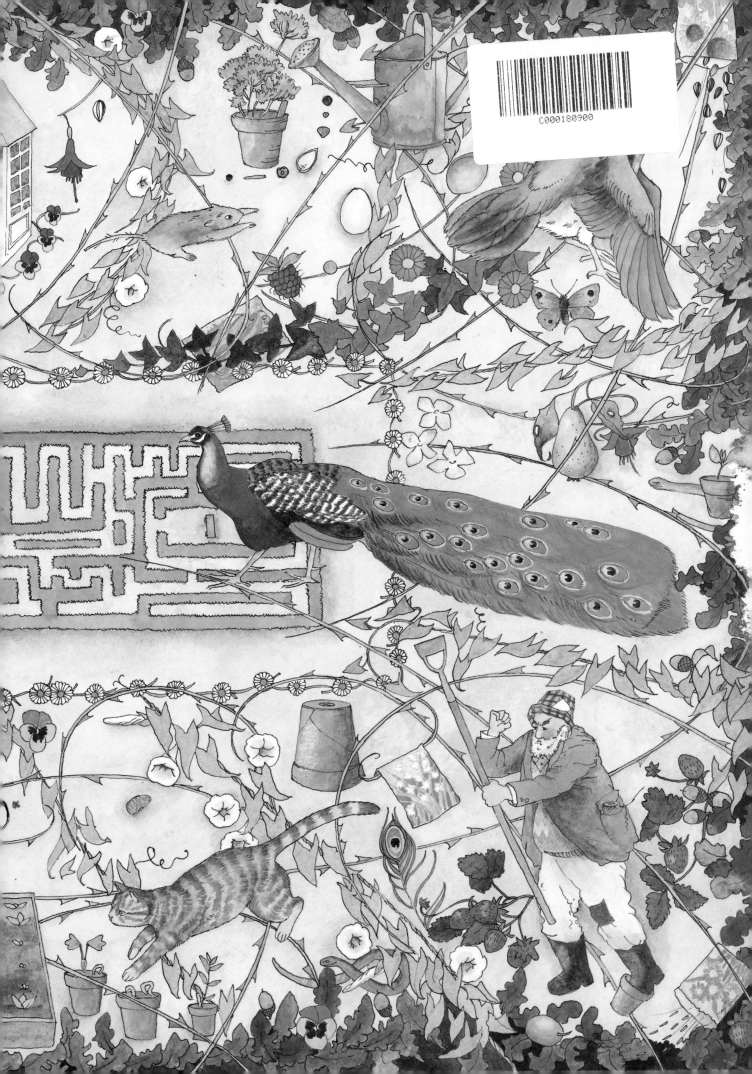

Catherine

For my friends in SNIP (LMJ)
For Zeki (MU)

British Library Cataloguing in Publication Data

Jennings, Linda M.
  Fred's garden.
  I. Title   II. Ursell, Martin
  823'.914 [J]   PZ7

  ISBN 0-340-39161-8

Text copyright © Linda M. Jennings 1987
Illustrations copyright © Martin Ursell 1987

First published 1987

Published by Hodder and Stoughton Children's Books,
a division of Hodder and Stoughton Ltd,
Mill Road, Dunton Green, Sevenoaks, Kent TN13 2YJ

Printed in Hong Kong

FRED'S GARDEN

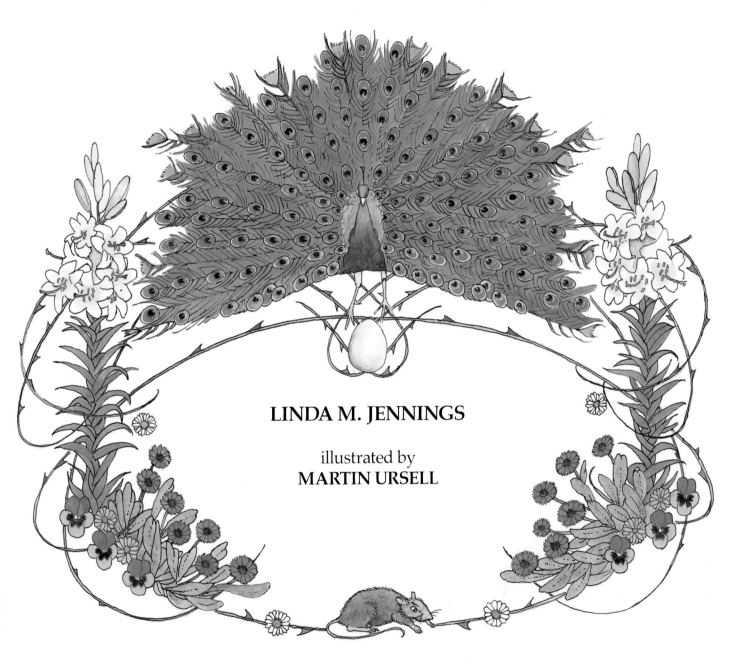

LINDA M. JENNINGS

illustrated by
MARTIN URSELL

HODDER AND STOUGHTON
LONDON SYDNEY AUCKLAND TORONTO

Once Fred had been an old lady's cat. He had slept on his own
cushion and eaten fresh fish each day. But that was a long time
ago, and now Fred lived in a draughty warehouse by the river,
rummaging through dustbins and catching mice for his supper.

One day, when Fred returned from hunting, he found a terrible scene. Big heavy lorries were rumbling over his favourite sunning spot, and the cardboard box that had been his bed lay squashed in the middle of a muddy puddle. His home was a pile of rubble!

Fred sat down and looked at the mess. He carefully washed himself from top to toe and thought hard. Then, with a flick of his tail, he set off to find a new home. Along the river-bank he went, leaving the factories and houses far behind him, until he reached the open country.

He went on and on, until at last he came to a huge gate set between two gate-posts with stone animals crouched on top of them. Fred thought the beasts looked a bit like himself.

"This is the place for me," he said, and squeezed through the bars of the gate into the greenery beyond.

Joyfully Fred sprinted along the smooth, wide, green pathway. It was a cat's paradise! To each side of the path there were tall trees and bushes stretching as far as he could see.

They were not like the trees in the Municipal Park. They were strange and many-coloured, and full of blossom. When Fred walked under them his ginger fur was speckled with petals, like snow.

Soon he came to a summer-house set amongst the trees. Under a wooden seat in the little house was a pile of sacking. This was just the place! Fred settled himself down, and slept.

Something had woken him! Fred sat bolt upright, his nose twitching. Then he saw it, a large, grey shape, streaking away from him under the summer-house, and disappearing into the bushes. Fred was after it like a flash. A rat would make a good meal.

He ran and he ran, through the bushes and out into the
open garden. Across a flower-bed he dashed, flattening the
plants as he went.

Then, from behind him, Fred heard an angry roar: "GET
OFF MY PLANTS YOU HORRIBLE GINGER CAT!"

A clod of earth followed it, hitting Fred on the back leg. The gardener at the Big House hated cats. In all his years there, he had made absolutely sure that never a paw nor a whisker would cross his beautiful flower-beds.

So when he saw Fred crushing his precious plants, his anger knew no bounds.

In the shrubberies and gardens there lurked a ginger cat – and that cat must be found!

It was not easy, for there were many places a cat could hide . . .

... and Fred was the master of disguise.

There was one place where the gardener never went, and this was the summer-house. Fred slept there on his pile of old sacks, and the rat lived under the floorboards. As Fred was too smart for the gardener to catch him, so the rat was too quick for Fred.

One day, when Fred was out exploring, he found himself on the peacock lawn. He had never seen a peacock before.

Fred liked birds, especially small, juicy ones, but this creature with its huge and brilliant tail was so amazing that he just sat and stared.

"That's all I need," said the peacock. "A common ginger cat with no manners. Be off with you – I have troubles of my own."

"Troubles?" said Fred.

"Yes, troubles," said the peacock. "Every time my wife lays an egg it is stolen. We should have a family by now," he added sadly.

"Do rats eat eggs?" asked Fred.

"How should I know?" said the peacock. "I never think about such creatures."

"Perhaps I can help you," said Fred, humbly.

Very early the next morning Fred was waiting for the rat.
And down by the gardening shed the gardener was waiting for
Fred. The rat slithered out from the summer-house, a grey
shadow in the misty morning sun. Stealthily Fred stalked it.

The rat crossed the flower-beds. Fred followed. And the gardener put down his hoe as he saw a ginger shape moving among the marigolds. "At last I've got you, you devil," he said and, on tip-toe, he crept after Fred.

Through the kitchen garden and into the shrubbery went the rat – straight to where the pea-hen was nesting.

"AAAK, AAAK, AAAK," screamed the pea-hen, as she fluttered away in alarm.

SPLAT! went the egg, as
the rat crunched it in his
jaws.

Fred sprang, catching the rat by the tail. The gardener
sprang, and grabbed Fred by the scruff of the neck. Grimly Fred
hung on to his prey, clutching at it with his paws.

Now, as the gardener hated cats, he was all for throwing Fred out of the grounds, rat and all, but the cries of the pea-hen had brought the owner of the Big House running out in his dressing-gown.

"That cat's caught the egg thief, Mr Cook," he said. "Let him go at once. A cat's just what we need around the place."

Fred is now part of the household. He can sleep on the
four-poster bed where once Elizabeth the First had slept.

He can curl up on the tiger-skin rug in front of a huge log fire. But his favourite place of all is on a pile of old sacks in his very own little house, deep in the woods.